宇宙の塵のためのブルース

The Blues
for the
Cosmic
Dust

JN123295

Anri Kang
姜アンリ

ポエムピース

宇宙の塵のためのブルース 暦

空を見上げる
全ての人たちへ

For all those who look up at the sky

4月
西の空、
宵の明星、月に近づく頃

April, in the western sky
When Venus approaches the moon

空
海
彷徨う惑星
青色巨星
ブルーシート
老いぼれのおでこの血管
そして
春の終わりに

世界の
あらゆる
ブルーを
見つける

露草
<ruby>露草<rt>つゆくさ</rt></ruby>
蒼穹
浅葱
瓶覗
青磁
瑠璃

群青<ruby>群青<rt>ぐんじょう</rt></ruby>

紺青<ruby>紺青<rt>こんじょう</rt></ruby>

電撃<ruby>電撃<rt>エレクトリック</rt></ruby>

真夜中<ruby>真夜中<rt>ミッドナイト</rt></ruby>

ブルーベリー

青い鳥

勿忘草<ruby>勿忘草<rt>フォゲットミーノット</rt></ruby>

これらブルーの中でも

もっとも

鮮やかな色

悲しみを

あこがれと

混ぜちゃったのが

あの焼けた空

In the sky
The ocean
Wandering planets
A blue giant
A tarpaulin
The veins of a senile forehead
And
The end of spring

Find
Every shade of blue in the world

Asiatic Dayflower
Azure
Light teal
Pale aqua
Celadon
Lapis lazuli
Ultramarine
Deep mountain
Electric

Midnight
Blueberry
Bluebird
Forget-me-not

Of these blues,
The most vivid,
Sorrow mixed with yearning,

Is that burning evening glow.

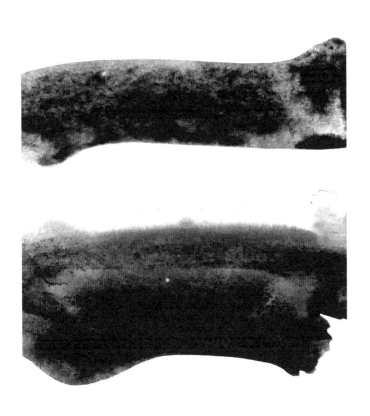

5月
たそがれ時

May
In the twilight

宇宙の塵のためのブルース

燃えている
燃えている

目と鼻の先で

燃えている
燃えている

農家のお家

真っ赤なお前が
木にぶら下がったまま
燃えている

道路を挟んだ
左手には
目を細めて
静謐
<ruby>せいひつ</ruby>

曲がり角も
脚と脚が交わるところで
燃えている

吐息が
重なるように
燃えている

抱かれたまま
ファスナー下げたら
びっくり真っ赤なお前が
逃げ出した

逸脱は
世界の寸前で
私とリチウムの炎を上げること

地上に焦げ落ちるお前は
まさに
ふわふわの

宇宙塵
涙なんてでないんだから
煙とガソリンの匂いで
いっそのこと
行方不明になってしまえば

そう
銀河の淵で
たたずんでいたら

足元で
咲いていたよ

空に焦がれる
ヒナゲシ

The Blues for the Cosmic Dust

Burning
Burning

Right in front of my eyes and nose

In flames
In flames

Is the farmer's house

Burning is
The crimson you hanging from the tree

On the left-hand side across the street
From the eyes squinting in suspicion
Stays tranquillity

Ablaze is
The street corner
Where pairs of legs are crossing each
other

Up in a blaze
Like how each gasp overlaps

Still held in your arms

I pull down the zipper
Out jumps lurid you
Fleeing in surprise

Deviation is
To burst into lithium flames
On the verge of the world with me

Burning topsy-turvy falling to the ash
Truly
You are fluffy cosmic dust

No tear would fall, right?
Why don't I just go missing in the
smoke and
The smell of gasoline?

Thinking so as I stand alone
In the depths of the galaxy

Just at my feet
I found it blooming

Pining for the sky
The Flanders poppy.

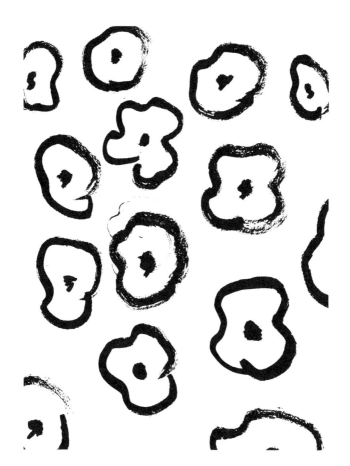

flanders poppies

梅雨
昼

The wet season
Lunchtime

ランチタイムというやつには
パリパリのクロワッサンと
とびっきりの逆襲が似合う

空は事実、
そう密告してくれた

首もとの汗がじわり

どうしてこうもちぐはぐで
どうしてこうもエクセントリック
ばらばらの空には
ひとりという鳥が
うんうんと群雲に
うな垂れていたのを
お忘れのよう

そんなのは御免だ
クロワッサンが空の下で
うな垂れる

ひとりというとりが
ひとりという
とりが
またひとり
灰色の雲になっていく

ひとりだって立派なとりだったはず

こうなったら仕方ない
お昼という姿に
告別式を開いてやると

そう言って
我慢ならないひとりが
また
ひとり
空へ消えていった

For something like
lunchtime,
a crispy croissant and a brilliant counter-attack
go splendidly.

In fact,
the sky informed me of that.

My neck sweats gently.

How can it be so incoherent?
How can it be so eccentric?
In the crumbling sky,
birds called Alone were
hanging their heads on the mass of clouds.
You seem to have forgotten that.

No, not that again,
said the croissant,
going soggy under the overcast sky.

Lone birds called Alone

turn into grey clouds
one after another.

Alone is supposedly a fine bird?
That's it.
I guess it's time to hold a funeral for so-called
'lunchtime',

said another Alone,
who could not bear this any longer,
and then vanished into the sky
alone.

ひとり
Alone

初夏
日盛り

Early Summer
In the heat of the day

きのうのことはないしょにしていてください。

かおをうずめてみたり、ぼくをそのままもっていっ
てしまったり。

やくそくは、あさ、ぼくと、そのなつのおそろしさ
のあいだだけにしよう。

じゆうから、ぼくを、すくってくれないかと

ひかげのなかで、ひっそり、あせ、かいている

こげてしまわないように！

Please don't tell anyone about last night.

Burying your face in me and
carrying me away like that.

In the morning, the promise
is just between me and the terror of summer.

Wishing
to be rescued
from freedom,
I'm perspiring
quietly
in the shadows—

without burning myself!

真夏
熱帯夜

Midsummer
A tropical night

蒸し暑い
東京の夜
ベランダの網戸
あ、
虫がいる
部屋のライトに照らされて
艶のある深みどりを
呈しているのが分かる
たぶん羽がある
人差し指ぐらいの虫だろうな
なんにも音はしないから
このひどい暑さに逃げてきたのかな
きっと羽を休めて夜をやりきろうと
この小さな網戸を選んだんだ
ゆっくり静かに這って
こっちを見ている気がする
艶っぽくて美しい虫だ
黒い羽があるかもしれない
でも飛びはしない
クワガタに似ているかも

黄金虫にしては大きいんじゃないか
どこからやってきたんだろう
近くにこんな虫がいっぱいいるんだろうか
網戸を眺めながら
ひとりベッドに横になって考えた
目がじわっと滲むと
金の背中も小刻みに輝いて
震えた

近くでセミが鳴き始めてる
こんな時間に

あれほど耐えられないものだったなんて
沈黙が

四方八方から襲ってくるのは
真夜中か

胸を締め付けているのは
ダボダボのTシャツ

虫、ベルベッドの表面を
左右に揺らしてる

一体どんな虫なんだろう
わたしと一緒に
こんな夜を過ごすのは

近くで見たい
ベッドから起き上がって
網戸に顔を近づける

ステンレスの小さな穴
白いしみが
薄くのびているのがわかった

A hot and humid
Tokyo night
On the screen door of the veranda
Ah,
There's a bug
Illuminated by the room light
I can see it gleams deep green
Maybe it's got wings
A bug the size of my index finger
It doesn't make any noise
So it might have come in to escape from this terrible heat
It must have chosen this small screen
To rest its wings to survive the night
It's taking each heavy but quiet step
And looking at me, I think
It's a beautiful bug with a sheen
Maybe the wings are black
But it doesn't fly
It looks like a stag beetle, perhaps
It is maybe too big for a gold beetle
I wonder where it came from
Are there many of it near here?

Gazing at the screen
Lying on the bed alone
I thought about the bug
As tears blurred my eyes
Its golden back flickered a little and
Trembled

Cicadas started singing nearby
At this hour of the night

I didn't know how unbearable it was
The silence

Coming to get me from all directions
Midnight

What's clenching my chest must be
This baggy old T-shirt

The bug, swaying its velvet surface
To the left and to the right

I wonder what kind of bug it is
To spend the night like this with me

I want to see it up close
Risen from the bed
I draw my face close

Across the stainless screen
I find
A thinly stretched white blotch.

8 月
薄暮

August
When daylight fades

夜が
自動販売機の
青い光
「つめた〜い100円」に
ひっそり囁いているよ

いい？
よーく見といて
今からわたし
ありとあらゆるものの中に
浸っていくから
ね

街灯の電流は黙り込む
ムシたちがバタバタと
羽をぶつけては消えていった

おばさんが昼間大事にしていた
外のひまわりも
もう口はきけない

暗黒分子に身をゆだねて
ほら
あのざまさ

さっさと帰宅する女の足だって
見てて
夜は得意げに
足首のところで
巻きついて
ひゅいっと
闇へ放りこむ

窓のカーテンなんてさ
昼間はそんなもの存在しないって
知らんぷりしてたくせに

熱を閉じ込めたまま
オレンジの照明で
包み込んだそれを
ガラス越しに

見せつけてくるんだから

唯一、夜だけには
秘密を漏らすことが
許されるかのように

月はね
その間
冷たいアルミニウムの窓枠に
つぐないを添えて
しずかに
艶めくときを楽しんでいたってわけ

こうやって
あらゆる隙間で
夜が勝利しているあいだ

みんな黙っていたんだ

自動販売機も

街のライトも、ムシも、ひまわりも
女も、カーテンも、窓枠も
月も

だけど
ただ1匹
猫だけが
ミャーッと叫んだんだ

よ。

The night is
Whispering into the blue light of the vending machine
—Cold 100 yen—

Ready?
Watch me
I'm going to soak into anything and everything, all right?

The electric current of the street lights falls silent
The bugs beat their wings then disappear

The sunflower outside
That the old lady took care of during the day
Was no longer able to speak a word
But has given itself up to the dark molecules
See
A pitiful sight

The woman's legs rushing home are easy, too
Look
The night proudly entwines around her ankles
And flings her into the darkness

The window curtains,
Although they ignored the existence of the thing during the day,
Now, with the heat shut inside, wrapped in the orange glow,

They show 'it' off through the glass
As *if it* was only the night
They could reveal their secret to

Meanwhile, the moon,
Bathing the cold aluminium windowsill in atonement,
Quietly enjoyed the alluring time

Just as the night prevailed
In each and every inch

Everyone hushed:

The vending machine
The streetlights
The bugs
The sunflower
The lady
The windowsill
And the moon

But a single cat
Cried

Meow.

夏の終わり
彼は誰時

The end of summer
Who-is-the-person-standing-over-there time
Daybreak

青い惑星

「お支払いは？
カード、現金、それとも…」
女のバイト (19) が尋ねた
すると男 (35) が震える小さな声で言った
「涙で」

女の眉間に
しわがより
辺りは一気に静まり返った

もう一度男は
「涙で払えますか？」
と呟いたので

女は言ってやった
「泣けよ、うんと泣け」

だから男はわんわん泣いた

44

やり切れない女もポロポロ
涙が頬をつたっていった

そうして
ふたり
一緒に泣いた

それを見ていた厨房のチョウくん
胸がキューってなって
ぽたりぽたり
床に大きな粒
落ちてった

どうしたもんか
途方に暮れて
シャツの袖で目元を押さえる
メガネは外れたまま
店長、
床にドンと崩れた
たまらなくなった客のオヤジも

なんだか悲しくて
うおうお泣いた

ついにオヤジの涙を拭うおしぼりも
やるせない
レモンサワーを道連れに
チョピチョピ泣き始めた

店中みーんな泣きだすもんだから
店、ぜーんぶ一粒の涙になって
こぼれた

それが沁みた朝5時の渋谷もたまんねぇ
ゴォーゴォーっとしずかに泣いた

涙ギチョ濡れになった渋谷に
いよいよまわりも我慢できなくなった

東京はずぶ濡れ
ホーカイはルイセン

ギャン泣きは鳴門海峡
知床半島の視界はにじみ
沖縄は今日も目頭が熱かった

日本中めいめいが
くしゃくしゃフェイスに
声を殺して
泣いた

ついに涙は溢れ出し
ソウルも
コルカタも
テヘランも
パリも
ブジュンブラも
アラバマも
プエルト・ウィリアムズも
フナフティも
こんな世に
皆、泣いた

やってらんねぇ
こんなことあってたまるか
どうしょうもねえ

ある者は
肩を抱きしめ合いながら

ある者は
闇に崩れ落ちながら

ある者は
休憩中、トイレの中
ハンカチで口を押さえながら

ある者は
走り叫びながら

またある者は
ひとり

布団にくるまったまま
誰にも知られないように

ついに涙は
溢れ出し
とうとう海になった

海は
どよめく声を上げて泣きながら
あらゆる地を
ゆっくり飲み込んでいった

地球は少し青くなったな

そんな地球を見て
月がうるっときた

The Blue Planet

'How would you like to pay?
Card or cash or...'
Asked the part-time girl (age 19)

Then the man (age 35) quivered in a
little voice,
'I'd like to pay with my tears'

The girl knitted her brow
Silence descended upon the bar

Again
The man murmured,
'May I pay with my tears?'

So the part-timer granted his wish,
'Go. Go ahead. Gush your tears'

He sobbed his heart out
Then teardrops
Trickled down the helpless girl's
 cheeks

So together

They cried

The kitchen guy named Cho
Looked at the scene
His heart cramped
Drip drip
Large drops splashed onto the floor

What's going on?
Powerless,
The manager wiped his eyes with his
sleeve
Glasses slipping off,
He slumped to the floor

Miserable,
The customer, a middle-aged salaryman
didn't know why
But he could only howl

Even the oshibori
The salaryman was using to dab his
tears away
Couldn't bear it any longer

Along with a glass of lemon sour,
It, too, started snivelling

As the entire bar burst into tears,
All of it became a single teardrop
And fell

Have mercy
With tears seeping through at 5am,
Shibuya silently wept

The neighbouring towns were next
One by one
They could not endure drenched Shibuya

Tokyo submerged
Lachrymal glands burst
Wailing is the whirling current
Of the Naruto Strait
Blurred is the view from
The Shiretoko Peninsula
Today, too, Okinawa is driven to tears

Crumpled faces all over Japan

Killed their voices
And cried

Eventually, tears flooded

Seoul
Kolkata
Tehran
Paris
Bujumbura
Alabama
Puerto Williams
Funafuti

Everybody grieved for the world

Why the fuck?
How could this be?
What do I do now?

Some
Holding each other's shoulders

Some

Collapsing in the darkness

Some
On a break, in toilet cubicles
Pressing handkerchieves onto their
mouths

Some
Running and screaming

And some
Under the duvet alone
So nobody could hear them

The torrent of tears
Swept down
And finally
Became an ocean

Bawling and roaring, slowly
The ocean swallowed everything far
and wide

The earth has turned a bit bluer,
hasn't it

Looking on
The moon was on the verge of tears.

The Blue Planet

秋
彼岸花、けっこう派手で
クラウドがクレナイに
染みこんじゃう瞬間

Autumn
The moment when red spider lilies are quite lit
and clouds soak into scarlet

やさしいってね、
この夏
萎むひまわりの眼差しのことだった

やさしいって
たぶん紫陽花のいちばん薄い青の部分
でも白ではないところ

やさしいって
クッキーのくずを口につけたまま
いとをかし
あの崩壊のこと

やさしいは
私の体温を奪ってもいいよ
だ

やさしいって
西の空に
オレンジとうすい青が混ざって

輝きながら消えていく割合

減数分裂は
やさしい

やさしいは
膨れた風船を突き刺す
あの細い細い針のこと

やさしいって
まだ名前のないこと

やさしいは
そよ風のことか

You know what is kind
How the withering sunflower glanced at us this summer

You know what is kind
Maybe the most pale-blue-
But-not-yet-white part of the hydrangea

Kind is
The collapse
How charming
When you crack up
With cookie crumbs around your mouth

Kind is
'You can steal my temperature away'

Kind is
The ratio of orange to pale-blue which fades away
While melting and shining in the western sky

Meiosis is kind

Kind is
The extra-fine needle that pierces
An inflated balloon

Kind is
When you don't have a name yet

Kind is
A soft breeze.

深まるころ
午後

A Deepening Time
Afternoon

、
、
、
、

きみは降ってくる猫
ぼくは落ちていくどんぐり
イチョウの血海へ
ふたり一緒に
砕け散るまえに
なんとか
消えなければならない

秋は
僕たちの重みに
耐えきれなかった

ただ
それだけのことだ

`
`
`
`

You are a falling cat
I am a dropping acorn
Before we both crash into the sea
Of Ginkgo blood
Somehow
We have to be gone

Autumn couldn't bear our weight

That was it.

冬
メトロ

Winter
The Metro

言葉で
完全に見失いたい
自分を
〜
〜
〜
もしきみが
真実を求める
腕のいい泳ぎ手だったなら
わかるはず
快速急行の風が
どうやって
肌に
切り込むか
この真夜中の
ひと気のない灰褐色の
プラットフォームで

口、開けな
遠慮はいらない

この地下鉄の空気
喰え

そうすれば
瞬時に理解するだろう

ああ
原子番号 10
ネオンが

魂に
光を灯してるんだった

I want to entirely lose track of myself
In words

~

~

~

If you used to be a good swimmer
Who seeks the truth,
You would know
How the wind of the rapid-express
Cut your skin
At midnight
In the lifeless dun
Of this platform

Do
Open your mouth
No hesitation here
This heavy underground air
Eat it

You will immediately comprehend that

Neon
The atomic number 10

Is indeed
Illuminating your soul.

12月
口に軽くナプキンをあてるきみと
22時21分の白いテーブルクロス

December
You are dabbing your mouth with a napkin
over a white tablecloth at 22:21

恋はきみの中で
骨になったよ

きみは立派な骸骨だ
踊ってください
わたしの前で

きみが包んでいるにんげんを
なんとか支えている
その素敵な骨たち

興奮する脊髄の奥には
寂しがり屋のニューロン
シナプスとシナプスのあいだを流れるのは

大空への弔意ひとつまみと
遠い銀河系への憧れ少々

仕上げに
母の不幸をひと振り

ほら
骨に染みた恋が
セーターを透かして
煌めいている

きみは惑星
ほんのり青く
ほんのり光る

きれいだ

Love has turned into bones inside you

Admirable bones,
Will you dance for me?

The nice skeleton that strains
To hold up the human within

Deep inside your stirred spinal cord,
Lonely neurones

Flowing between synapses,
A pinch of condolence for the sky and
A dash of longing for a galaxy far, far away

To finish,
A sprinkle of your mother's misfortune

You see,
Love, which has melted in your bones,
Is emanating through your sweater

You are a planet
Slightly blue
Slightly shimmering

Beautiful.

1 月
彗星がやってくる夜

January
Night with a shooting comet streaking across the sky

ここに
悲しみポテトチップスあらわる！
のり塩は、遠いエーゲ海のソルトやないんや
あの大阪湾の
どす黒いエメラルドグリーン
腎臓にガツンと来るような磯の香り
そんな風味や

アパートの小さなふとん
かき分けてすすんだとこ
窓開けて顔出したら
見えるんは
工場の白い煙と
雲の縫い目を照らす
ブルーライト
USJ が天に放つ
アメリカの光

約束は
果たされへんまま

プカプカおっちゃんが浮かぶ
淀川やった

悲しみポテチ
子どもの靴の裏で
パリパリッ
最期の音立てる

寒いなぁ
白い息昇ってく
子ども
ポケットに手突っ込んで
バリバリ悲しみポテチを後にした

もう
ここには
戻らへん

そう呟いて
あっちのほうへ

燃えてった

Here they are
The sorrow potato chips!
This 'Seaweed and Salt' flavour doesn't contain
Salt from the far-off Aegean Sea
But from the menacing dark emerald green
of Osaka Bay
The sea aroma that gives your kidneys a knockout blow
That's the fucking flavour

A tiny duvet in a minuscule apartment
Ploughing your way through the clutter
Opening the window
Leaning out

You see white smoke from the factories
The seams of the clouds glorified by the blue light,
The American light
Universal Studios
Shoots at the sky

The promise—repeatedly broken—was
Yodo River where the old man was floating

The sorrow potato chips make their final sound
Crunch
Under the back of a kid's shoes

It's cold
Frosty breath rises into the air
The kid shoved her hands into her pockets
And left the crunchy sorrow potato chips behind

'I will never come back'
Muttered the kid
Then burned into the far,
far distance.

The Sorrow potato chips

2 月
東の空、そっと焦げてしまうころ

February
The eastern sky, softly burning

浮遊感のあるソファーに
あなたの顔と銀河の渦を
浮かべて
全身をうずめてみる

それで

X218

そこに
宇宙人と交信する
穴を発見するのだ

4.Q91.3

何十億年
細胞分裂を繰り返しても
伝達されてしまう
この物忘れと
小指の震えは

宇宙人と交信するときの
唯一の手がかりとなる

わたしが
この銀河ソファー Z7-02 の中に
小さなブラックホールを望む
悲しい
にんげんのひとりだと
思い出すための

5・333・3
670. 8
3
460.3

宇宙人と
目と目で交信するときは
今まで聞いたことのない
リズムが
パパパパパパパッパ

星くずになって流れるんだ

そしたら
私たち
粒子になって
飛び跳ねる
時の瞬きになって
金色に縁取った真っ赤なレーザー
浴びるんだ

にんげんだって
ちいさいものが
だいすきなのさ

胸がうずいて
熱くなったり
冷えてしまったり
するのも嫌じゃない

さあ

準備はいい？

目と目を合わせて

<ruby>4<rt>フォー</rt></ruby>
<ruby>444<rt>フォーフォーフォー</rt></ruby>
<ruby>4444444<rt>フォフォフォフォフォフォー</rt></ruby>

わたしを
そっちにつれていって

On the sofa, feeling like I'm floating in the air
I imagine your face and the Milky Way
and sink into it.

Then,
X218.

There
I discover
a hole
through which to communicate with aliens.

4.Q91.3

This forgetfulness and these shaky pinkies,
still inherited after billions of years of
repeated cell division,
will be the only clues
in communication with the aliens
to remind myself—
I am just one helpless human being
wishing for a small black hole
on this galaxy sofa Z7-02.

5 · 333 · 3
670. 8

3
460.3

When you communicate eye-to-eye with aliens,
you hear rhythms that you've never experienced before—
Pah-Pah-Pah-Pah-Pah-Pah-Pah-Ppa
drifting in stardust.

We spring up
as we turn into particles.
Be the blink of a moment
bathed in a bright red laser with a golden rim.

Humans love little things, too.

We don't mind our hearts getting hotter or colder from aching.

Are you ready?

Look into my eyes.

4
444
4444444

Now take me over there.

～願わくは花の下にて春死なん
その如月（きさらぎ）の望月（もちづき）の頃～ *
雪の降らない朝

-Let me die in spring under the cherry blossom trees
around the time of the full moon in March-
The morning with no snowfall

* — 西行の歌より

泡雪と小春

おい、
夜が肌に雪崩れ込んできた
そういうことだろ？

花の匂いも嗅げねえ、情けねえやつだ
そう思ってんだろ？

凍った高層タワーの
エントランスホールに
そのまま
忘れてきたんだろ？

いいえ
あなた
忘れてなんかいませんよ
夜にくるんで
持ってきたわ
あなたのところ

57 階に

ほら
あなたの好きな
沈丁花の香りもいっしょに

でも
よかった
あなた

雪、
もう少し
溶けていたら

雪、
わたしになって
泥と一緒に
消えていたところです

The Slush and The Small Spring

Hey,
The night has collapsed into my skin,
am I correct?

Bet you think
I'm a miserable fool, who can't
even smell the flowers, don't you?

Bet you've left it in the entrance hall
of the frozen skyscraper
and have forgotten all about it, haven't you?

No, darling,
of course, I remember.
I've brought it wrapped in the night for you,
here to the 57th floor.

See, darling?
I've also brought your favourite flower fragrance with it,
winter daphne.

But darling,
I'm glad.

The snow
if it had melted a bit more,

the snow
would have been me
and faded into the mud.

3月
昼下がり

March
Early afternoon

春風が吹いたある午後の日

シドニー・ラニアーが言った

「音楽は言葉をさがしている愛だ」

でもそれなら重すぎる

だから永遠に愛のまま

空を飛び回ってくれればいい

言葉を諦めてしまった小鳥のように

あとは少しだけスカートをめくって

陽気におどりながら目の前に現れて

心の奥のフックに一つでも引っかかるように

でも

あなたの言葉でこのおどりは完成されないし

このおどりであなたは完成しないのだ

もし音楽が言葉をさがしている愛だったら

どうか、言葉を探している愛よ

言葉なんかすっぱり諦めて

そのまま私を突っ切って下さい

それこそ本当に

風が

音楽になる時なのだから

One afternoon when a spring breeze was in the air

Sidney Lanier said,

Music is love in search of a word

But then, that's too heavy

So please waft around in the sky

As love forever

Like a bird

Which has given up on words

Then catch the hem of your skirt a little

Reappear before my eyes dancing merrily

So something gets hooked in the depths of our hearts

But your words

Won't complete this dance

And this dance won't complete you

If music is love in search of a word

Please love in search of a word

Abandon words gracefully

And gust through me

Because

That's when the wind

Truly becomes music.

Cherry blossom Petals

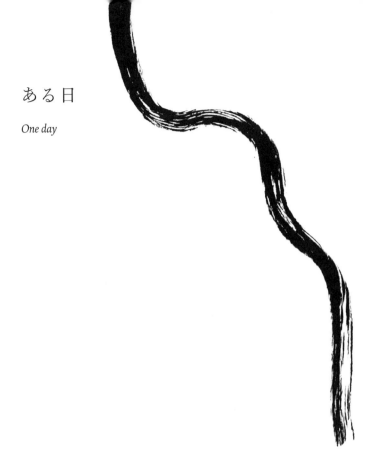

ある日

One day

～～～～～～～～～～～～～～～～～

あなたはどんどん消えてゆき
私はどんどん入っていく

気づいたら、

外、

一光

～～～～～

~~~~~~~~~~~~~~~~

You are vanishing
and I
am drawing in
further and further.

Then notice,

outside,

— light.

~~~~~

たった今

Just now

女でもなく
男でもない
アフリカ人でも
日本人でも
人間でもなく
動物でもない
機械でもなく
鬼でもなく
お化けでもなく
無論、
紙でも神でも
花でもなければ
恋人でもないし
売り手でも
買い手でも
創造者でも
創造されたものでも
子供や大人
母や父
誰かの娘でも息子でもない

導く側でも
また
導かれる側でもない
システムでもなければ
記号でもなければ
歴史でも
未来でも
粒でも
波でもない

こうやって全て身を投げつつ
受けてもなしに腐ってゆく

あなたから
全て剥ぎとって残るもの

滲みでる
廃物液として
流れ込んできてください

Not

A woman

Nor a man

Nor an African

Nor a Japanese

Nor a human

An animal

A machine

A demon

A ghost

Clearly

Neither kami nor kami

Nor a flower

A lover

A seller

A buyer

Not a creator

Nor a creation

Not a child nor an adult

A mother nor a father

A daughter nor a son

Not a leader
A follower
A system
A symbol
No, not history
Nor future
Not a particle
Nor a wave

But something,

Throwing its entire self off as it
Rots away being received by nobody,
That is left in you after everything has been stripped off,

An oozing slurry

Please flood into me.

空と海が
秘色で
繋がっていたころ

In the days when the ocean and the sky were linked
by the secret colour, celadon

魂が春を売るのはよいとして
それより私が気になるのは
春が魂を売ったりはしないだろうか
ということ

一途に膨らんだ芽に
ドキッとしたのだ

快楽は柔らかくて
すぐ手の届くところに
生えているんだから

あなたは心地のよい日
芽を見て言った

そして若葉をピリッと割いて
脇道に捨てた

きみどりの先からは
濡れた鉄の匂い

原始
世界は春だったんだろう

人々は
眠りから半分覚めて
口の上下運動によって発せられる音に
金色に思考するパビリオン
優しい電流の匂い
速攻除菌系、愛のグルーヴ
高層タワーは永遠に傾眠傾向
うごめく恥骨の付加価値
危ない存在の料理学

こんな勝手な予想を立てては
あきらめなかった

繋いできたものを
途絶えさせるものか
手放すものかと

ただ、それだけだった

原始、世界は死んでいく春

それはこの地の母でありつつも
みんな母に抱かれていたころ

肉も土も花も海も熱も
ぜんぶ繋がっていたから
風は
なんとも言えない匂いがして
味は窒素と誇らしさがマリネした
息つまる辛酸の蜜
それでもって耳元で
「まわれ、まわれ、まわれ」と
囁くのだから
頬はもう、
ちょっと熱くなって
からだが望むがまま
踊るしかなかった

けっして
忘れるものか
閉ざすものか
落ちてゆくものかと

心臓から発せられる偶然に
電子が走り
手拍子を打つ
声を遠くへ狂わせ
まだ出会っていない
こどもたちのことを思って
グルーヴを飲み込み
土を踏んだ

原始、世界は春だったのだろうか

夏、
ちいさきものたちが一斉に愛し合い

秋、
それぞれが世界の淵を染めていった

冬、
心地よい眠りが辺りを包む

そして
次第に
みんな
落ちていった

下へ
下へ

落ちていった

それぞれの速さで
赴くままに

下へ

下へ

落ちてゆきながら
みんな踊った

全てを忘れて
また
思い出すために

枝には柔らかい芽
風はなんとも言えない匂い
味は窒素と誇らしさがマリネした
息つまる辛酸の蜜

頬はもう、
ちょっと熱くなって

胸の奥は痛んだ

I don't mind if a soul sells spring
I'm concerned about
Whether spring sells a soul,
Or not

I felt a thrill
At the buds blooming intently

Pleasure is soft and
It grows within your hands

On a lovely day
You said so
While nipping the tip off a fresh twig
Before casting it away into the gutter

From the tip of the lemon-green
Drifts the scent of
Wet iron

Originally,
The world was spring
I supposed

People were half-risen from their sleep
To the sound delivered from the up-
and-down

Movement of a mouth
They made these self-indulgent
assumptions:
The pavilion that thinks in gold
The gentle smell of electric currents
The groove of love that instantly
sterilises all
The skyscraper forever inclined to
somnolence
The added value of the wiggling pubic
bone
Culinary science of dangerous beings

And they never gave up

To never let die
To never lose anything
They have inherited
That was all

Originally,
The world was a dying spring

That's when we were mothers of the
land
But at the same time
Were all embraced by mother

Flesh, soil, flowers, sea, and heat,
They all blended
So the wind smelled unfathomable
The taste was a marinade of nitrogen
and pride,
The nectar of pungency that suffocates
Besides, it whispered in your ear,
'Turn, turn, turn'
Your cheeks already
Felt a little hotter
You had no choice
but to dance as your body desired

Wishing
Never to forget
Never to shut off
Never to fall

Electrons run
Clap your hands
To the chance
Beating from your heart
A wild cry stretches far
Thinking of the children you had yet to
meet,
Swallowing the groove,
You stepped on the soil

Originally the world was spring
—Or was it?

Summer
Small creatures loved each other all at
once

Autumn
Each of them dyed the world's abyss

Winter
A pleasant sleep enfolded everywhere

And
Gradually
Everyone
Fell

Down
Down

They went

Each of them
At their own speed
In their own way

Down
Down

They fell
And danced

To forget everything so that
They can remember it again

Soft buds on the twigs
The wind smells unfathomable
The taste is a marinade of nitrogen and pride,
The nectar of pungency that suffocates

The cheeks already
Felt a little hotter

Deep down
The heart ached.

おわりに

ブルースは青色で、憂鬱、大陸を渡ってきたあの頃の記憶を呼び起こす脈拍――、世の中を生きながら「どこか欠けている何か」を感じている空を見上げるすべての人々へ捧げる、今を歌い漂うための言葉です。

テクノロジーがどれだけ人間社会を発展させようとも、宇宙とのつながりを祝いながら、人間がbluesを歌い続けること、これを切に願います。

初めての出版にあたり、無名の私を拾って最後まで導いて下さったポエムピースの谷郁雄編集長、ならびに近藤美陽さん、素敵な仕上がりにして下さったデザイナーの清水美和さん、本書に関わって下さった全ての方々に、この場を借りて心から感謝を申し上げます。英文のチェックは私の長年の友人である、サッカージャーナリストのショーン・キャロル氏に助けて頂きました。本当にありがとうございます。

そして日頃からお世話になっている方々、仲間たち、いつも伴走してくれる竜也に深い感謝を。

姜アンリ

姜アンリ ── Anri Kang

1990年、京都市生まれ。
中学卒業後ニュージーランドのダニーデンに留
学、オタゴ大学で演劇と社会学を学ぶ。日本に
帰国後、東京都内で英語講師として活動しな
がら、からだと言葉、日本語と英語の波打ち際
をめぐる詩の創作に取り組む。
好きな空間は縁側と海辺。

宇宙の塵のためのブルース

2023年4月24日 初版第1刷

著　者	姜アンリ
発行人	松崎義行
発　行	ポエムピース
	〒166-0003
	東京都杉並区高円寺南 4-26-12 福丸ビル6F
	TEL 03-5913-9172　FAX 03-5913-8011
編　集	谷郁雄
装　丁	清水美和
イラスト	姜アンリ
印刷・製本	株式会社上野印刷所

© Anri Kang 2023 Printed in Japan
ISBN978-4-908827-79-2 C0092